The Ghostly Tales of Mr. Tooth

Gerald Holt

Cover and text illustrations

David Smith

Riverwood

Copyright © 1992 Gerald Holt

Riverwood Publishers Ltd.
6 Donlands Avenue, P.O. Box 70, Sharon, Ontario L0G 1V0

P.O. Box 78306, St. Louis, MO 63178

Canadian Cataloguing In Publication Data

Holt, Gerald
    The ghostly tales of Mr. Tooth

ISBN 1-895121-13-2

I. Title

PS8565.048G46 1992   jC813'.54   C92-094668-2
PZ7.H64Gh 1992

Illustrations by David Smith
Design and typesetting by Heidy Lawrance Associates
Printed and bound in Canada by Webcom

Cover illustration dedicated to the memory of Edith A. Smith

Contents

CHAPTER ONE
Mr. Tooth

Hal shivered. He hated being the last to leave school. He glanced back at the old stone building. On misty evenings like this it had a ghostly atmosphere. He shivered again, peering through the fog anxiously, hoping that his father wouldn't be much longer.

"Hello there."

Hal almost jumped out of his skin. He hadn't seen the school crossing guard.

"Waiting for your dad again?"

Hal nodded. "He won't be long. He should be here any time now." Hal didn't know the crossing guard. He'd seen him on a few evenings during the last week, but he'd never spoken to him.

The old man smiled. As he did so one of his middle top teeth dropped down. It rested on his lower lip. Hal was so startled that he took a step back. The old man chuckled. "It's only my false tooth; nothing to be frightened of."

"Oh." Hal wasn't sure what he should say.

"The crossing guard smiled. "A lot of children have called me Mr. Tooth because of it." Hal watched fascinated as the old man spoke. The tooth bobbed up and down with every word. "You can too, if you like."

Hal thought about this. He remembered the crossing guard at his last school. He was a fat round man. He had the biggest feet Hal had ever seen and his enormous shiny black boots made them seem even bigger. His name was Mr. Smith, but Hal had thought of him as Mr. Feet. He hadn't called him that of course. Although Mr. Feet had been fat he was not a jovial person. In fact he was very strict. Now this guard was saying that it would be fine to call him Mr. Tooth. Hal looked at the old man. He was still smiling. He was the opposite of Mr. Feet. He was very thin. His hat, with the red band and shiny black peak, was too big. It rested on his ears, folding them over slightly. With his tooth on his lip and his ears bent over he really looked quite funny. Hal wanted to laugh. He stopped himself and looked down. The old man had shiny black boots like Mr. Feet, but these boots were very small.

"Well then? What do you say?" The crossing guard smiled down at Hal.

For a moment Hal forgot what they'd been talking about. Then he remembered. He smiled back and nodded. "Okay, Mr. Tooth."

"Right." Mr. Tooth looked at his watch. "Your dad seems to be a bit later than usual."

Again Hal nodded. He wished his father would hurry up. It was a nuisance not being able to take the bus like the others.

"I'll wait with you if you like," said Mr. Tooth. "I don't have anything better to do at the moment."

"Thank you," said Hal. He was glad the old man was staying. He looked back at the school. The fog was thicker, or perhaps it was just getting darker. But the old stone building had taken on an eerie gray look. He shivered and looked away.

Mr. Tooth smiled. "Looks rather spooky on a night like this." He chuckled. "With Hallowe'en just over a week away I expect you youngsters are thinking more and more about ghosts. What are you planning on being this year?"

Hal hadn't really made up his mind. He'd been a spaceman last year and the year before that he'd gone out as a vampire. That had been fun. With the mask no one had known who he was. He shrugged. "I don't know. I've never dressed up as a ghost."

"What?" said Mr. Tooth. "Never been a ghost. That's half the fun."

"Well," said Hal. "I wouldn't know what type of ghost to be anyway."

Mr. Tooth nodded. "Maybe I can help you there. I know a few ghostly tales."

"About real ghosts Mr. Tooth?"

"Well some are and some aren't." Mr. Tooth smiled. His tooth rested on his lip.

"I don't believe in ghosts," said Hal. "Not real ones."

"Ah, I see." Mr. Tooth nodded and then twisted first one end and then the other of his straggly gray moustache. "Lots of people don't. But one in ten people see one and it's usually people who don't believe that do. Some don't see them of course, they just hear them or feel them."

Hal shivered. Even though he didn't really believe in ghosts, he didn't like to think about them. He thought about the times he'd felt as if someone was behind him. He remembered one time when he was sure there was someone and he'd whirled round. There'd been no one there. Maybe he was one of those people who could feel ghosts. He shook his head. That was dumb. There weren't real ghosts.

Mr. Tooth was still smiling. "You really don't believe in ghosts, do you?"

"No," said Hal emphatically. "But you can tell me some ghostly tales if you want to. It might give me some ideas for Hallowe'en."

"Okay then." Mr. Tooth nodded. "But not now. Here comes your dad. Come and see me tomorrow and we'll see what we can dream up."

"Okay, Mr. Tooth. Thanks for waiting with me." Hal waved and ran towards his father's car. "See you tomorrow."

"Okay, son. Bye." Mr. Tooth was swallowed up in the mist.

Hal climbed into the car. "Hi, dad."

"Hi, son. Sorry I'm a bit late. Who were you waving to?"

"The school crossing guard, Dad. He waited with me till you came."

Hal's father looked in the mirror and pulled slowly away from the kerb. "Hm. That was good of him. I didn't notice him in all this fog. I'm glad he's around though, particularly on a night like this."

"So am I, Dad," said Hal. "So am I."

CHAPTER TWO
The Big Hairy Hands

The next day, Hal waited until the other children had left the school. He wanted to have Mr. Tooth all to himself. Many of his new school friends were discussing what they would be on Hallowe'en night, but none were going out as ghosts. Until he'd decided Hal didn't want anyone else knowing what he was thinking. He looked out of the door. It was misty again. The school yard looked something like a huge white cloud with a chain link fence floating round the edge. At first Hal couldn't see his friend. Then he saw him by the gate. Mr. Tooth was rubbing his hands together to warm them. Hal waved and the old man waved back. He beckoned for Hal to join him.

Hal ran across the yard ."Hi, Mr. Tooth," he said breathlessly.

"Hi, son. Another foggy night." Mr. Tooth nodded slowly. "Reminds me of the hairy hands. Big hairy hands they were."

Hal smiled. He'd thought about ghosts last night and spoken to his brother about them. Mike was thirteen, two years older than Hal. He'd laughed and by the time they were ready for bed, Hal had no more doubts. There were no such things as ghosts.

"What reminds you of the hairy hands, Mr. Tooth?" asked Hal.

"This weather, this mist. It's like the mists they get back home on Dartmoor." Mr. Tooth nodded solemnly. "The hairy hands," he repeated. "Hairy hand weather this is."

Despite himself Hal shivered. It was the way Mr. Tooth said 'the hairy hands' that did it.

"A curse they were. Ghastly. Terrifying." Mr. Tooth pursed his lips and shook his head. "Don't know if I should tell you."

"Is this a real ghost story or a make-believe one?" asked Hal.

Mr. Tooth twisted the ends of his moustache. "I thought you said you didn't believe in ghosts."

8

Hal shrugged. "Well I don't really. But you said yesterday that some of your stories were about real ghosts and others not."

"That's true, I did." Mr. Tooth winked. "Well I'm not telling you whether this one's true or not. You must decide for yourself." He stroked his moustache and took a deep breath. "I didn't always live in Canada. I came here from England when I was a young man. It was when I was on my way here that I was haunted by the hairy hands, on Dartmoor as I said."

"What's Dartmoor?" asked Hal.

"Dartmoor?" Mr. Tooth took a deep breath. "A bleak rocky place that is; a place of moors and bogs filled with bones of centuries past; and some new bones too." He paused. "That's why the prison was built there. It's where they put the worst criminals, murderers, violent men." He shook his head. "Many a prisoner has died trying to escape from Dartmoor; stealing off into the mist, thinking they were free, only to be sucked down into the mud and slime of a bog." When the old man said the word 'sucked' his false tooth sank down below his lip and then bobbed up. "And many a traveller has been lost too, swallowed up, never to be seen again." Mr. Tooth shook his head. "I didn't want that to happen to me, I can tell you."

"Were you alone, Mr. Tooth?" Hal found himself whispering; he didn't know why, but it seemed the right thing to do.

"All alone," said Mr. Tooth. "All by myself, in the dead of night too."

"Why?" asked Hal. He couldn't think why anyone would be alone on a misty night, in a place where there were bogs, and the bones of centuries past.

"I hadn't meant to be there," said Mr. Tooth. "I was on my way to Plymouth to catch a boat to Canada."

"Why didn't you catch a plane?" asked Hal.

Mr. Tooth chuckled. "Had to be rich to catch a plane in those days. I had to come by boat." He stroked his moustache. "But as I was saying, I didn't mean to be out on the moor road, not with the curse of the hairy hands having struck again just the week before." He looked round as if someone might be listening.

"What do you mean, Mr. Tooth?" Hal found himself whispering again. "What was the curse of the hairy hands? What happened?"

"Well," said the old man. "Some said the hairy hands belonged to a stoneage man, sucked down into the bog thousands of years ago. Others said they were the hands of the murderer Dirty Jack Dodds. He escaped from Dartmoor prison before he could be hanged."

"Did he die in the bogs, Mr. Tooth?"

"He did, son. He did." Mr. Tooth sighed. They set the dogs after him as soon as they knew he was gone. It was a dark misty night like this. The dogs soon picked up his scent and went howling and barking into the night. The wardens and the police followed, carrying lanterns. It must have been eerie, the lanterns swaying this way and that, the dogs howling in the mist."

Hal nodded. He could almost feel he was there.

"When they got to him he was almost gone," said the old man. "The reports say that all that could be seen were his hands, big hairy hands they were, clutching, grasping at the mist above the deepest bog on the moor. Then they sank out of sight."

"Wow. That's awful," said Hal.

"An evil end for an evil man," said Mr. Tooth. "And his evil's been haunting the place ever since."

"How?" asked Hal.

"I don't know that I should tell you," said Mr. Tooth. "It might scare you."

"Psaw." Hal tried to laugh. "It's only a story isn't it?"

"That's for you to decide, son." Mr. Tooth looked very grave. "Okay, I'll tell you. You see nobody ever saw Dirty Jack so the hands might not be his. They might be the hands of a stoneage man or a person sacrificed hundreds of years before. They did that in those parts. But every so often a traveller will be haunted. In the old days coaches were turned over, horses led into the marshes. Always there were reports of the hands rising out of the mist. Then it was people in cars; they'd be driving along when these big hairy hands would come thudding down on the windows all round them. The hands would claw at the glass with ear piercing scratches."

Hal shivered. He felt goose bumps rising on his arms and he glanced around nervously.

"Then just the week before, a lady had been driving on the moor road. When she didn't arrive home on time her husband went in search of her. He found her unconscious at the wheel of her car. She'd crashed into an old tree, one of the few on the moor. When she recovered all she could remember were the hands clawing at the glass. She hadn't been able to see properly. She'd driven off the road. Lucky the tree was there, because just beyond that spot is a very deep bog."

"Wow," said Hal. "But what happened to you?"

"I was coming to that." Mr. Tooth nodded slowly. "As I told you, I was heading for Plymouth to get a ship to Canada. It left the next day. I was trying to save money and a friend offered to drive me. But as we came to the moor, just before nightfall, his car broke down. He couldn't get it going, so I decided to head off on foot. My friend thought I was crazy."

After hearing about the hands, Hal thought Mr. Tooth was crazy too.

"But I had to keep going, even if I walked all night." Mr. Tooth adjusted his hat. It sat a little further back now but still pushed his ears down.

"So off I set. As cars came along I tried to thumb a ride."

"Mum and Dad have told me not to hitch-hike," said Hal. "It's dangerous."

"They're right," said Mr. Tooth. "And as it happened I had no luck at all. No one stopped for me. The mist was getting thick and I don't really blame the drivers. Finally I needed a rest. There was a tree by the side of the road and I sat down on my pack and rested my back against the trunk. I must have dozed off for a while, because the next thing I knew a car had stopped on the road. I could just make out the shape through the swirling mist The lights glowed dimly. The driver must have seen me. I jumped up, opened the passenger door and reaching behind me to grab my pack, climbed in. As I went to shut the door what do you think I saw?"

Hal had been holding his breath, waiting. He let go his breath with a gasp. "I don't know, Mr. Tooth. I don't know."

"I'll tell you." The old man paused, looked round, then back at Hal. "I'll tell you. The inside of the car was as misty and damp as it was outside. It was cold, ice cold, deathly quiet. It was empty. And slowly the car started to move forward. As it did there was a grunting moaning sound—'agh, agh!' And there on the steering wheel was a hand."

"Was it a hairy hand?" Hal could feel the hair on the back of his neck stiff against his collar. "Was it hairy?"

"I couldn't tell," said Mr. Tooth. "You see it was covered in…"

"Mud," blurted out Hal. "It was covered in mud wasn't it; mud from the bog."

"Was it the ghost then?" asked Mr. Tooth.

"Of course it was," said Hal. "It had to be."

The old man started to chuckle. He shook his head slowly. "No son, it wasn't the ghost of the hairy hands. It was a man whose car had run out of gas—petrol we called it. He was pushing it and had stopped to get his breath when I woke up. But I yelled blue murder when I saw that hand. I frightened him too. At first he thought my yelling was the screams of Dirty Jack. We had quite a laugh about it as you can imagine."

Hal looked at Mr. Tooth. He was a bit annoyed. Although he didn't believe in ghosts, the hairy hands had sent a creepy feeling down his spine. He looked at the old man. As he chuckled the tooth bobbed up and down.

"Sorry about that, son. But I did say that some of the tales would be about real ghosts and others not. Anyway, here comes your dad. See you tomorrow."

CHAPTER THREE
The Bell Ringer

"So?" said Mr. Tooth. "Did you decide to be the Hairy Hands on Hallowe'en night?"

Hal shook his head. "No. I don't think that would be too good. Anyway, you didn't see a real ghost, Mr. Tooth."

"No," said the old man, "that's true. But lots of other folk did."

"How do you know that Mr. Tooth? Suppose they all thought they saw a ghost, like you did, at first."

"Well son, that's one way of looking at it." Mr. Tooth twirled his moustache. "But if a person says they've seen a ghost, who is to say they haven't; there's no way to disprove it; they know what they saw—or felt." He rocked back and forth on his tiny feet.

Hal was about to ask why the old man's feet were so small when he thought he'd better not.

The crossing guard was talking again.

"Maybe I should tell you about Egbert the bell ringer."

"Egbert!" said Hal. "What kind of name is that?" He started to laugh.

Mr. Tooth snorted. "There's nothing funny about the name Egbert. It's a good old English name. In fact my great-grandfather was named Egbert."

"Sorry, Mr. Tooth," said Hal. "It's just that I'd never heard it before."

"Well I don't know that I want to tell you the story now. First you don't believe in ghosts; now you laugh at people's names." Mr. Tooth shook his head. "I don't know."

"Oh please, Mr. Tooth." Hal was angry with himself. He wanted to hear the tale of the bell ringer.

"Well alright then," said the old man sharply. "But no laughing, you hear?"

"I promise Mr. Tooth."

"Right—well—Egbert the bell ringer." Mr. Tooth looked down at Hal. Hal still thought the name Egbert was funny but he kept his face straight.

"It was when I was a boy. We lived in England.

I sang in a cathedral."

"What's a cathedral, Mr. Tooth?"

"What's a cathedral? Why, it's a huge church of course. There's always a bishop in charge. Smaller churches just have vicars or priests or ministers. Bishops are senior to them."

"Oh, I see." Hal nodded. "Why are there bishops?"

Mr. Tooth shook his head. "Never mind that. The thing is that I sang in this cathedral and I saw the bell ringer."

"How old were you, Mr. Tooth?"

"Eleven I think, or maybe twelve." The old man twisted the ends of his moustache. "About your age."

"How old was he?" asked Hal.

"How old was who, son?

"The bell ringer, Egbert," said Hal.

"I don't rightly know," replied the old man. "He'd been dead about four hundred years. I don't know how old he was when he died."

"Oh. So this is a real ghost story."

"Yes it is, son. And I'll tell it, if you just let me begin." Mr. Tooth nodded slowly and pressed his lips together. The ends of his moustache seemed to droop in the cold damp air. "I was down in the crypt when I first saw him."

"What's a crypt?" asked Hal.

"Dear me," sighed Mr. Tooth. "Don't you know anything? A crypt is a large area under the main floor of a cathedral."

"Sort of like a basement?" said Hal.

"Yes, in a way." Mr. Tooth looked round and lowered his voice. "In the old days, hundreds of years ago, that's where they buried people, especially important ones like bishops. Sometimes they buried them under the floor under huge slabs of stone. Sometimes they put them in table tombs."

When the old man said the word 'tombs' he made it long—'tooooooooombs'. It sounded eerie. Hal looked round. He shivered. He wanted to ask what a table tomb was, but he wasn't sure if he should.

"I might as well tell you what a table tomb is," said Mr. Tooth. "I doubt you'll know what it is. It's like a huge stone box or coffin built up from the floor. On top there's a thick slab of stone, the table top. And sometimes there's a stone carving of the person inside, lying on the table."

21

Hal shivered again. He tried to imagine being in a huge basement with graves under the floor and skeletons in big stone boxes all round. "Why were you down there?" he whispered.

"It was my job, son." We kept all the music down there and when we'd finished singing for the night I had to collect it, take it down and put it away tidily. Then I'd change out of my cassock and…"

"What's that?

"Now what?" said Mr. Tooth testily.

"A cassock," said Hal. "You said you…"

"Tut, tut." The old man shook his head. "A cassock's a long black coat reaching to the ground. And before you ask, I also had a surplice. That's a white gown or cloak. Anyway on this particular night I'd changed and I was racing up the stairs from the crypt. I didn't like to be down there by myself. When I reached the top step I realized that all the lights were out. The verger—and before you ask, that's a man who looks after the cathedral—must have thought I was gone. He'd locked up. It didn't matter though, the moon was shining through the stained glass windows and I knew my way around. The side door had a latch I could open to let myself out." Mr. Tooth paused as if remembering that night.

"What happened, Mr. Tooth?" Hal knew that the old man had seen the bell ringer but he wanted to know what happened then.

"When I reached the top step I heard the wind. It was blowing a real gale out there. There were whistling noises and moans all around. I knew that was only from the wind, but just the same it sent shivers down my spine." The old man shook himself. "It was terrible. It was as if all the bodies in the graves were crying out, calling to me. I knew they weren't of course, but I was scared."

Hal started to shiver. It must have been horrible.

"Then it started," continued the old man. "Clang, clang,—clang, clang. It wasn't the sound of the bell I knew. But it just kept on ringing— clang, clang,—clang, clang. And I knew what it meant you see."

"What did it mean?" whispered Hal.

Mr. Tooth nodded solemnly. "I knew," he repeated. "We all knew about Egbert the bell ringer. When he tolled the bell someone was going to die. It always happened."

"But, how did you know it was Egbert?" asked Hal. "It could've been the wind making the bells ring."

"No," said the old man. "I told you it wasn't the usual bell and then besides, I saw him. The bells stopped and I saw him coming towards me. He wore a thick black cassock and a hood. But he had no face. I knew it was him."

"How?" said Hal. "How did you know it was Egbert if you couldn't see his face?"

"Because he came from his tomb, you see." Again Mr. Tooth drew out the word 'tomb' and Hal shivered. "He was buried in a table tomb, near the top of the stairs to the crypt. I'd often seen it and like the other boys I'd rubbed the head. They said it brought good luck. But over the years, hundreds of years since he was buried, with people rubbing his head like that, his face had been worn away."

Hal imagined the table tomb and the faceless image on top; and then the ghost in the black cassock with the empty hood. He started to say something but the old man was continuing.

"Then the dog started to bark, right outside

24

the door. It howled and scratched at the old wood. I thought, if I could open the door and let the dog in the ghost couldn't get me. I ran as fast as I could, but when I got there, he was there before me, his back to the door, the hood shaking from side to side."

Hal felt his throat go tight. "What did you do?" His voice came out as a croak. He swallowed hard.

"What did I do? What would you do? I ran. I ran as fast as I could, down the aisles, round the pillars, until I came to the front doors. The two main doors were shut fast, but the small door to the right was wide open. The ghost of Egbert was there holding it for me, beckoning me through. I was running so fast I couldn't stop and I was out into the night before I knew it."

"Wow!" exclaimed Hal. "That was a narrow escape."

Mr. Tooth nodded. "Yes, it was. As I came outside the wind buffeted me this way and that. But above the roar of the wind I could hear the bells and then the howling of the dog. Suddenly the howling stopped and there was a crash from round the side of the cathedral. People were

gathering and they started to run towards the noise. I followed them." Mr. Tooth shook his head. "It was a terrible sight."

"What was, Mr. Tooth?"

"There was a dog by the side door. It was a huge dog, savage to look at, but gentle. You see I knew the dog. It belonged to the organist. A massive tree had fallen beside the door, the door I would have left by. And under the tree was the organist, dead of course. His dog lay beside him, whimpering and crying."

"Phew." Hal shook his head. "It could've been you. Mr. Tooth. If you'd gone out that door it could've been you."

"That's right, son. When I told my story, I learned more about the bell ringer. They said that if you just heard the bells you might be the one to die. But if you saw him as well, then he had come to rescue you."

"Wow!" exclaimed Hal. "Wow! Maybe I'll go out as a bell ringer. Just maybe."

"Well, here comes your dad." Mr. Tooth pointed at the approaching car. "Don't decide just yet. You might want to go out as Old Samuel. Now off you go. See you tomorrow."

CHAPTER FOUR
Old Samuel

"Now who was I going to tell you about tonight?" asked Mr. Tooth.

"Old Samuel," replied Hal promptly. You said not to choose Egbert until you'd told me about Old Samuel."

"So I did, son. So I did." Mr. Tooth smiled and his tooth dropped onto his lip. "Old Samuel was a poacher around our way. Not when I lived there, but about a hundred years or so before I was born."

"Is this another story about when you were a boy, Mr. Tooth?" asked Hal.

"Yes it is, son." The old man nodded. "But I was a few years older than when I met Egbert the bell ringer. Now, you know what a poacher is, don't you?"

"Oh yes. A poacher's someone who goes out

with a gun and kills animals without a licence." Hal had watched a television program recently about people poaching bighorn sheep and caribou.

Mr. Tooth nodded and stroked his moustache. "That's partly right, son. But not all poachers use a gun; most didn't in Old Samuel's day. In fact they didn't use guns at all. Guns make noise and the poachers wanted to be as silent as possible. They didn't want to get caught by the gamekeeper."

"You mean the Game Warden don't you, Mr. Tooth?" It was a Game Warden that had narrated the television program about poaching.

"No, son. I said gamekeeper and I meant it. You see the big land owners in Britain didn't want people stealing their rabbits and pheasants and deer and suchlike." The old man smiled and nodded, his tooth bobbing up and down on his lip. "They wanted all the sport for themselves. So they had these men called gamekeepers who were in the woods at night trying to catch the poachers. They still have them."

"What happens if someone's caught?" asked Hal.

"Well nowadays, not too much." The old man

took a deep breath. "But in the days when Old Samuel was a poacher they might be hanged or ..."

"Hanged!" shouted Hal. "You mean executed and killed?"

"That's right, son." Mr. Tooth nodded. "If they were lucky they were deported."

"What's that?"

"Deported?" Mr. Tooth smiled. "Boy, you need to learn a thing or two. Deported means being sent overseas, never to come home again. They mostly sent them to Australia. That's what happened to Old Samuel."

"Then how did he become a ghost?" asked Hal.

"That's what I'm going to tell you isn't it. You see, he's known as Old Samuel because he wasn't caught until he was an old man. He'd been a poacher all his life, hunting in old Squire Bodkin's woods since he was a boy. He must have caught hundreds of rabbits in his time."

"How did he catch them?" asked Hal.

"Same as I did," said Mr. Tooth. "With a snare on the path that the rabbit used. My father taught me."

"You mean your father was a poacher too?" said Hal.

The tooth bobbed up and down as the old man laughed. "Of course he was. So was my grandfather and my great grandfather Egbert. His grandfather, my great great great grandfather was taught by Old Samuel himself." The old man paused. "Maybe it was his son, Young Samuel. Anyway, it doesn't matter, that's how I learned."

"Boy," said Hal, "weren't you scared?"

"Never." Mr. Tooth was very emphatic. "Well, only that one time of course."

"When was that?" asked Hal.

"If you'll just let me get on with the story I'll tell you." Mr. Tooth stroked his moustache and rocked back and forth on his feet. "When Old Samuel was caught it broke his heart; not because he'd been caught, but because he was sent to Australia. He loved the countryside where he'd grown up. He'd never been anywhere else, never wanted to go anywhere else. He just wanted to live and die in the village and be buried in the church yard." The old man nodded sadly. "But he never was, you see. He was sent to Australia. Word has it that he died a year later. But he did return in the end."

"How do you mean, Mr. Tooth?" Hal wondered if someone had brought Old Samuel back in his coffin for burial. He'd heard that sometimes happened.

"Well," said the old man, "after he was tried and sentenced, Old Samuel swore he'd be back. He said that even if he died his ghost would return and haunt the gamekeepers of Bodkin woods. And he did return and he still haunts the woods."

"Was it his ghost that scared you Mr. Tooth?" Hal was beginning to wonder if there really were ghosts after all.

"No, son." The old man smiled. "It wasn't Old Samuel that scared me. But he sure scared someone else." He nodded and chuckled. "It was Jackson he scared."

"Who was Jackson?" asked Hal.

"Jackson was the gamekeeper when I was a boy. " Mr. Tooth stroked his moustache. "Big man he was, and mean too. And he was sneaky." The old man nodded slowly. "Half the rabbits and pheasants poached in the woods he took himself. Many a time I saw him set a snare himself." Mr Tooth chuckled. "Half the time I didn't set my own snares, I'd just go round to his before he did. I didn't take all the rabbits, only what we needed for a good stew or a pie."

Hal started to laugh. "Did he know what you were doing?"

"No," said Mr. Tooth. "And if I'd just kept to that everything would've been fine. But Mum and Dad were talking one day about a big family reunion. Mum said it would be nice to have something special for dinner instead of rabbit or pheasant or trout from Bodkin river."

"You mean you couldn't go fishing either?" Hal could hardly believe his ears. He loved to go fishing.

"Not in Bodkin river, or the streams." Mr. Tooth shook his head. "Had to be a friend of old Bodkin, or pay very high to belong to his club."

"I think that's rotten," said Hal.

"So did I, son." The old man smiled. "But we had our fair share of fish I can tell you. Anyway, I got to thinking about this family reunion.

There'd be my grandparents, and lots of aunts and uncles and masses of cousins. Half of them I couldn't remember their names. So I thought it would be wonderful to have venison for dinner."

"You mean you were going to snare a deer Mr. Tooth?"

"Well not exactly, son. I intended to shoot one." Mr. Tooth held up his hand. "I know what you're going to say, so hold on. I wasn't going to use a gun. I had a bow and arrows. I thought I'd try my hand. So early one morning there I was, hiding in the woods where I'd seen deer. I hadn't been there more than ten minutes when I saw one. I drew my bow and took aim. The arrow flew and I lost sight of it. But the deer fell."

"Wow," said Hal. "What a shot."

"What a shot indeed," said Mr. Tooth. "I waited for a while and then crept forward. As I bent down to look at the deer I realized that it wasn't my arrow that had struck it. Then there was a bellow behind me and Jackson came charging out from behind a tree. His face was twisted in anger and I turned to run. But I tripped over the deer."

Hal could almost feel the fear that Mr. Tooth had felt as a boy. He held his breath and waited.

"There I was on the ground," continued the old man, "and Jackson almost upon me. But he wasn't looking at me for some reason. He jumped over the deer and ran past me. Then I heard him scream. It was enough to make your blood freeze. I lifted myself up on one elbow and turned. There he was, held fast by the throat. An old, old man held him and was shaking him. 'Told you I'd be back, Ned Jackson. Well here I am, Old Samuel come to pay you a visit.'

"It was his arrow, wasn't it, Mr. Tooth?" Hal knew he was right.

The old man was nodding. "I'll tell you about that in a minute. First let me finish telling you about the game keeper. It turned out you see that when Old Samuel was caught it was an ancestor of Jackson who caught him, Ned Jackson. Anyway, Old Samuel let go of the game-keeper. Jackson just stood there as if he was a statue and the old poacher helped me drag the deer away and hide it. But before I could thank him he disappeared. I ran all the way home. I told my dad what had happened but he wouldn't believe me. So I took him back to the woods. There was the deer, the arrow still in it. My dad took out the arrow carefully. He was shaking and refused to say anything. He grabbed my hand and we ran home so fast I could hardly breathe."

Hal waited. The old crossing guard was breathing heavily, shaking his head. Finally he calmed down. My dad sent Mum for one of Old Samuel's relatives. They were back in minutes. The lady that came took one look at the arrow and asked where Dad had found it. It had belonged to Old Samuel, you see."

"Boy, that was a great story, Mr. Tooth." Hal smiled. "I bet that gamekeeper had a shock."

"I was just getting to that, son. Jackson never recovered his senses. When next he was seen he was wandering round the village muttering 'Old Samuel, Old Samuel.' I heard tell he died a few years after I came to Canada. Some say his ghost haunts the woods now, wandering down the trails. Some people see him, others just hear him. He shouts in fear and then starts mumbling, 'Old Samuel, Old Samuel'.

CHAPTER FIVE
The Lady in Black

Hal woke up on Monday morning glad that the weekend was over. It was the first time he could remember actually wanting to go to school. As his dad drove up to the old stone building Hal looked eagerly for Mr. Tooth. He was disappointed when he didn't see the old man. Hallowe'en was just five days away and he hadn't decided on a disguise.

As the day wore on Hal found that he couldn't concentrate on his school work properly and he kept looking out of the window. His classroom faced the road and he watched for the old man. Then it started to get foggy and as school ended all was gray and drab and heavy with damp. Hal hurriedly put on his coat and dashed outside with the other children.

"Hal! Hal Bates!" It was Mrs. Anheim the

librarian.Hal turned back. The teacher was smiling, holding a book. "My, you're in a hurry. I found a book for you, about ghosts."

Hal remembered that he'd been looking for a ghost book at lunch. He looked at the title— 'Ghostly Tales for Hallowe'en'. There was a picture of a witch on the cover.

"Thanks, Mrs. Anheim." He glanced towards the road. "I have to go and wait for my Dad."

The teacher nodded. "Okay, Hal." She smiled. "And don't frighten yourself with all those spooky stories."

Hal shook his head. "I won't. I don't believe in ghosts, I just want some ideas for Hallowe'en."

"Fine then. See you tomorrow," said the teacher.

"Bye, Mrs. Anheim." Hal turned and ran across the yard. He stopped at the gates. There was no sign of old Mr. Tooth. Hal was upset. He'd looked forward to seeing the old man again. He wandered down to the crossing and stood under the street light. Idly he thumbed through the pages of the book.

"Well hello, son." Hal jumped. It was Mr.

Tooth. He closed the book and looked up. The old man smiled. "Thought I'd missed you tonight."

Hal shook his head. "The librarian found me a book. I was talking to her."

"Ah, I see." Mr. Tooth lifted his right eyebrow slowly. "Good book, is it?"

"I don't really know yet, Mr. Tooth."

"What's it about then?" asked the old man.

Hal felt a bit awkward. Here he was with a book about ghosts and he'd told Mr. Tooth he didn't believe in them. He looked at the book and then showed it to the old man.

The crossing guard chuckled and his tooth bobbed up and down. "Don't believe in ghosts, eh!" He laughed. "Well that book won't help you. Witches aren't ghosts."

Hal felt his face turning red. He put the book in his bag. He wondered if Mr. Tooth believed in witches as well as ghosts.

"Witches are one thing, ghosts another," said the old man. "But seeing that picture of the witch reminds me of the lady."

"The lady?" said Hal. "What lady, Mr. Tooth?"

"The Lady in Black, son. The Lady in Black."

The old man nodded slowly. "Terrible tale it is."

Hal felt his flesh crawl. It was the way Mr. Tooth said 'terrible'. It wasn't the first part of the word but the last—the 'ible' bit. It seemed to roll into the fog and become part of it.

"Terr—ible it was," repeated Mr. Tooth. "Do you want me to tell you?"

Hal nodded in spite of himself. He wasn't sure that he really did want to hear about the Lady in Black.

"Well, this happened when I was a young man. I had so many experiences with ghosts that people came to ask me about them. I became known as a ghost expert." The old man nodded. "I remember it well. There had been reports in the newspapers—headlines. 'Lady In Black Seen Again.' 'Man Goes Mad After Seeing Black Gowned Lady.' 'Three Men Run In Terror From Haunted Mansion.'" Mr. Tooth nodded again.

Hal waited while the old man paused in thought. He wondered who the Lady in Black could be and what Mr. Tooth had done.

"The Lady in Black was a rich widow," said the old man. "Her husband had left her a huge fortune, but she was mean and miserly and wouldn't spend a penny if she could help it. She was so mean, that after her husband was gone, she never wore anything except the black dress she'd worn to the funeral. And even that she'd worn to many funerals before.

"Wow, she really was mean, wasn't she," said Hal.

Mr. Tooth nodded. "She was so mean that she dismissed all the servants except one, the old cook. And it was said that she beat the cook with a broom if she cooked two potatoes instead of one, or caught her feeding scraps to the birds. Having dismissed all the servants, the house was never cleaned, the grass was never cut, nothing was ever repaired. And gradually the trees and bushes became overgrown, crowding in toward the house. No one would go to the house, but people who passed by at night reported hearing blood curdling screams and fiendish laughter. The cook used to come down to the village to shop each week. She bought the cheapest meat; stale bread; soft potatoes; she bought anything that was cheap."

"But why did she stay with the Lady in Black?" Hal looked up at the crossing guard. "I wouldn't stay with someone who beat me with a broom and never got any decent stuff to eat."

"Ah, but you see, the cook was waiting for the old woman to die." Mr. Tooth nodded solemnly. "She thought that the Lady in Black had left her a pile of money in her will. Some people will do anything for money you see."

"I wouldn't," said Hal.

"I agree, son. Money's not everything." The old man stroked his moustache. "And the cook never did get any money anyway. She died before the old lady died. One day she was in the village shopping when she walked under a ladder. You should never do that, now should you?"

"My dad says that's just superstition," said Hal. "You're not superstitious are you, Mr. Tooth?"

"Well, some of us are and some not." The old man nodded. "Maybe the old cook should've been and walked round the ladder."

"What happened?" asked Hal.

"There was a bricklayer up the ladder." Mr. Tooth drew in his breath sharply. "Whoosh!" the sound came out so strongly that Hal jumped back. Mr. Tooth raised his right hand and then brought it down sharply. "Whoosh!" he repeated. "Down came a brick right on the old cook's head. Stone dead she was."

"Boy," said Hal. "After putting up with all that rotten food and stuff at the mansion."

"Right," said Mr. Tooth. "And not two days later the old lady died too. The vicar went up to the house to talk to her about burying the old cook. He didn't go by himself, he took a crowd with him. The old lady was in her dining room, a pile of jewels and money on the table. She screamed at them; said no one could stay in her house; told them to get out. Then she grabbed the broom and raised it over her head. She died of a heart attack."

"Were you there Mr. Tooth? Did you see her die?"

"No, no." The old man shook his head. "I told you, I was asked to investigate her ghost. You see, nobody could stay in that house, just as the Lady in Black had said. When anyone bought the house they never stayed more than a week. The Lady in Black would scare them out of their wits."

"What did she do?" asked Hal.

"She'd throw saucepans around. If there were

more than two potatoes in a pot only two would cook. The others would stay hard." The old man set his lips in a thin grim line. "One lady who was cooking was beaten with a broom."

"Wow!" exclaimed Hal. "She just couldn't stop being mean, could she."

"No." Mr. Tooth shook his head. "But worst of all she would wake people up in their beds, scream at them, tear the bedclothes off. So, I was asked to stay in the house one night. It was believed that if I could stay there, then she would be beaten, because she'd said no one could."

Hal looked at the crossing guard in awe. There was no way anyone would get him to sleep in a haunted house, not with a ghost like that. He suddenly realized that he was now starting to believe in ghosts. He waited.

"So I made my preparations." The old man nodded solemnly. "I had six candles and three flashlights—torches I called them then. I had several books to read, funny ones. I had two flasks of tea, four packets of sandwiches and a gun. Then I set off." Mr. Tooth paused and looked round. He lowered his voice. "I found a nice bedroom to stay in and settled down. I'd just finished my first sandwich and a cup of tea when the candle I'd lit went out. I switched on a flashlight and tried to relight the candle. It wouldn't light. So I took another and lit that. After about five minutes an icy wind filled the room and the second candle went out. It wouldn't light again."

Hal shivered. If he'd been Mr. Tooth he'd have left right then.

"The same thing happened with all the candles." Mr. Tooth shook his head. "I couldn't get any of them to stay alight. So I tried reading with a flashlight. It hadn't been on more than a minute before it went dead. The others didn't work either. I was a wee bit worried I can tell you."

Hal was standing looking at Mr. Tooth in amazement. If that had happened to him he'd have been more than 'a wee bit' worried. He would've been terrified.

"Then it started to get cold, icy it was." Mr. Tooth nodded and then smiled. His tooth rested on his lip. "So I snuggled down between the sheets. I felt under the pillow where I'd put

my gun. I kept my hand there and waited. The house was deathly quiet, the only noise was the creak of the springs as I shifted in the bed. Well, I must have dozed off because the next thing I know is that I'm shivering, cold as a steak in the freezer. The moon was shining through the bedroom window. Everything was still, but for some reason I felt a ghostly presence."

Hal grasped his bag tightly. He felt very cold even though he was wearing his thick parka. "What happened?"

Mr. Tooth looked grim. "I took a firm grip on my gun. Then I looked round." He shook his head. "There at the end of the bed were two enormous hands."

"The hairy hands?" gasped Hal.

"No, son." Mr. Tooth shook his head again. "Two big white ghostly hands."

"What did you do?" Hal almost shouted.

"What would you have done? I shot them of course. 'Bang! Bang.'

Hal waited. The old man was sighing, looking down.

"The pain was terrible son, just terrible."

"What pain Mr. Tooth? Did you get her? Did

you? What happened?"

"I got her all right." Mr. Tooth laughed. "I stayed there all night; couldn't move. You see, those weren't her hands I'd shot. I'd shot off my toes."

Hal couldn't believe his ears. The old man had tricked him with a make-believe story. Then he started to laugh. It would be great to tell Mike this one. He was still laughing when he looked at Mr. Tooth's feet. They were very, very small.

CHAPTER SIX
The Dancing Bear

"Have you decided then?" asked Mr. Tooth as Hal joined him after school the next day.

"No," said Hal. "I was wondering. All the stories you've told me are about ghosts in England. Don't you know any Canadian ghost stories?"

Mr. Tooth stroked his moustache and rocked back and forth on his tiny feet. "Hm. I haven't met any ghosts here in Canada myself, but..." he paused for a second. "There is one story I know. It's a story about a bear."

"A bear?" said Hal. "You mean the ghost is a bear?"

"That's right," said the old man. "Lots of ghosts are animals, you know; cats and dogs, all sorts of things."

Hal shook his head. "I thought ghosts were

only people.

Mr. Tooth smiled. "Well," he said, his tooth bobbing up and down. "Do you want to hear the story of the bear?"

Hal nodded. "Yes please, Mr. Tooth."

"Right. This happened to the grandfather of a friend I made when I first came out here. Maybe it was his great grandfather." The old man took off his hat and scratched his head. Hal had never seen Mr. Tooth without his hat. The old man was bald and his head was very shiny and very white. In the mist it looked like a shiny white beacon. The crossing guard put his hat back on and his ears folded back down. He nodded. "I remember now, it was his great grandfather. He was a Hudson Bay man at Fort Langley."

"Fort Langley. Wow," said Hal, "that's only a few miles from here."

"That's right, son." Mr Tooth continued. "He lived at the fort when old trapper McTavish was there."

"Who was trapper McTavish?" asked Hal.

"He was the owner of the bear," said the old man. "He'd found it in the forest near the fort."

Hal couldn't remember seeing a forest near the fort when he'd visited with the school. Mr. Tooth seemed to read his thoughts. "There used to be forests all over, before the logging started, and then people settled here and farmed the land. Anyway, old McTavish found the cub. It's mother was dead."

"So the mother bear was the ghost," said Hal.

"No, no, no," said Mr. Tooth testily. "Don't interrupt or I won't tell you the story."

"Sorry, Mr. Tooth." Hal wanted to hear this tale. He couldn't think what a bear ghost could be like.

"Well, as I was saying. Old McTavish found this cub. He took it back to the fort with him as a pet. McTavish didn't do much trapping any more. He made a living by pressing and baling the furs that the Indian trappers and others brought to the fort to sell to the Hudson Bay Company." Hal remembered seeing the big wooden press in the grounds of the old fort, so he could imagine old McTavish placing the beaver pelts in the press and bundling up the furs.

"When he wasn't doing that he worked in the

company store." Mr Tooth smiled. "And when he'd finished his work he would play the bagpipes. The bear cub would sit and listen to old McTavish playing the pipes and one evening it started to dance. McTavish had an old kilt and he put this on the bear. The people at the fort would come and watch the bear dance as McTavish played. Trappers and loggers and settlers would come too and McTavish and his bear became famous. The bear learned to do other things. It would juggle wooden balls; it did balancing tricks; but best of all people liked to watch it dance. The folks in those days didn't have much to entertain them. They didn't have television, or movies, or radio or even a theatre. So they would gather and watch and clap as McTavish and his bear entertained them. And they gave the old trapper money. In fact he made more money this way than he ever did trapping."

Hal tried to imagine McTavish standing in the grounds of the fort, the bear dancing to the music of the bagpipes.

Mr. Tooth continued. "Well, as I said, McTavish was an old man. One day he died. The

governor of the fort wondered what to do with the bear." Mr. Tooth sighed. "A young man, another Scotsman, had envied old McTavish making all this money. He told the governor he would look after the bear. It was agreed. This greedy young fellow also took the McTavish bag-pipes. But he wasn't very good." Mr. Tooth shook his head. Hal waited.

"Well you can imagine what happened." The crossing guard sighed again.

"The bear wouldn't dance, would he?" said Hal.

"Quite right, son." The old man nodded. "That bear wouldn't dance for that greedy young scalliwag. And the man got angry. He beat the bear, he starved it, he chained it up. But the bear wouldn't dance or juggle or do bal-ancing tricks any more. Then, one day, right outside the company store, it happened."

"What happened?" asked Hal.

"I was just going to tell you." Mr. Tooth twisted the ends of his moustache. "The bear got angry. The young man was prodding it with a pointed stick, trying to make it jump. Well it did jump, right on top of him. It wasn't a cub any more, but a full grown bear." Mr. Tooth shook his head. "Everyone said that the bear didn't intentionally kill its new owner. But as it landed on the young man there was a snap. The man lay dead, his neck broken."

"Oh, no," said Hal. "So they killed the bear."

"No, that's where you're wrong." Mr. Tooth looked sternly at Hal. "Now listen and I'll tell you the rest."

"Sorry, Mr. Tooth. I just thought they'd kill the bear for having done that."

The old man shook his head. "As I told you, the people knew that the bear hadn't killed the young man on purpose. It just wanted him to stop torturing it. And they knew that he'd been cruel since he'd become the owner. But some of them were worried just the same. So they locked the bear in a shed while they decided what to do. The bear cried and cried. Another Scotsman— there were a lot of them at the fort in those days—tried to quieten the bear by playing the McTavish pipes. He was better than the young man and the bear stopped crying. But every time the man stopped playing it started to moan and cry again."

Mr. Tooth stopped and stroked his moustache. He continued. "Night came. The mist rolled up from the river. The piper played on. There was a young guard on duty that night. He was close to the shed and he started to hum to the tune the piper was playing. Without warning the door of the shed crashed open and the bear stood there, it's eyes gleaming in the moonlight. The young guard was terrified. He raised his gun and fired. With a cry of pain the bear clutched it's chest, staggered forward and then fell to the ground. It was dead."

Hal felt a lump in his throat. He knew the bear had to die or there wouldn't be a ghost. But he was still sorry.

"Nobody blamed the guard, of course," said Mr. Tooth. What else could he have done. So the bear was buried, but you can still see him in the governor's house today. That rug on the floor in the office is the McTavish bear."

"But that's not a ghost," said Hal. "I thought you said this was a ghost story."

"Did I say I was finished?" The crossing guard sounded angry. "I've a good mind not to tell you the rest."

"I'm really sorry, Mr. Tooth. It's just—well, it was so interesting—and then you said that about seeing the bear at the fort—and…"

"I know, son." The old man nodded. "It could sound like the end of the story, I suppose. Okay then, I'll tell you the rest." He took a deep breath. "Now I told you that my friend's great grandfather was a Hudson Bay man. He worked at the fort a few years after McTavish and his bear were buried. One night he was on guard. Up and down he marched, round and round past the store and up to the shed. He was standing near the shed smoking his pipe, humming a tune. 'Da dee dum dum dum, da dee dum dee da.' It was a lovely summer night. But for some reason he felt cold. He warmed his hands on the bowl of his pipe and continued to hum. 'Dee da do do dee, dee da la dee da dee do.'

"As he turned to start his patrol once more, he noticed smoke coming out from under the door of the shed. He was about to raise the alarm when he felt an icy wind which seemed to freeze him to the spot on which he stood. The smoke poured out, rising in front of him. And then the smoke turned black and started to move this way and that. And he saw the bear, it's eyes gleaming, it's forepaws raised, standing on it's hind legs. He was terrified. He raised his gun and fired. The bear came towards him. He fired again, but the bear was almost on him. He didn't have time to reload, so he fixed his bayonet on the end of his rifle and charged. He ran full tilt at the bear, straight through it and hit the door of the shed. His bayonet stuck fast in the wood and he couldn't pull it out. He turned to face the bear and as he did so he heard the sound of bagpipes. The bear was dancing. 'Da dee dum dum dum, da dee dum dee da.' It was the tune he'd been humming."

"Wow," said Hal. "All the bear wanted to do was dance to the tune."

"That's right, son." Mr. Tooth nodded. "I've never tried it myself. But I bet if you went out to the fort at night and hummed that tune, the bear would come."

Hal thought about that. Maybe when he was older.

CHAPTER SEVEN

The Phantom of the Orchestra

The next evening, Hal crossed the street. Mr. Tooth was waiting. "I thought about about being the bear," said Hal, but I ran into a problem."

"Oh, what was that?" asked the old man.

"Mom got mad when she found me in her fur coat. It's only an old coat my grandma gave her." Hal shook his head. "But Mom said if she caught me in it again I was for it."

Mr. Tooth chuckled. "You might think it's only an old coat because it belonged to your grandmother. But it's probably worth a lot of money."

Hal nodded. "That's what Mom said. It's a mink, or something like that."

"Ah," said the old man. "I can see why she was upset. Mink coats are worth a fortune." He sighed. "My mother had a coat like that. It wasn't a mink, but she only wore it on special occasions." Mr. Tooth smiled. "It reminds me of the Phantom of the Orchestra."

"Don't you mean the Phantom of the Opera?" asked Hal.

"No, son." Mr. Tooth shook his head. "This phantom haunted concert orchestras. It didn't haunt all the players on the same night or at the same time. It seemed to choose one player, usually someone giving a solo."

"What did it do?" asked Hal.

"I was just coming to that," said the old man. "It did different things to different people, but the result was the same. If someone was giving a violin solo the phantom might jog their elbow. There would be a terrible screech. Or if it was the pianist, the phantom might play some extra notes that sounded ghastly." He nodded. "I was told that one time he stood in front of the trumpet player sucking lemons."

"Why did he do that?" asked Hal.

Mr. Tooth smiled. "When you suck lemons in

61

front of a trumpet player or a trombonist it makes their mouth go dry and their lips quiver. It's the worst thing you can do. They can't make the notes properly."

"I don't see how someone sucking a lemon can make your mouth go dry," said Hal. "Mine wouldn't."

"Oh yes it would, son." Mr. Tooth nodded and rocked back and forth on his tiny feet. "Have you ever scratched a blackboard with your finger nails?"

Hal smiled. "My cousin hates me doing that. She can't stand it."

"Right," said the old man. "It doesn't send shivers down your spine, but it does send them down hers."

"It's true," said Hal. "If someone does it to me I get shivers and my teeth hurt." He looked at the crossing guard. "But I didn't know that about lemons."

"Well, that's what sucking lemons in front of a trumpeter does." Mr. Tooth laughed and his tooth bobbled up and down. "Anyway, I was telling you about the phantom. You see, my mother was wearing her fur coat the night we went to the concert. When you mentioned your mother's coat, it reminded me." The old man sighed and took a deep breath. "It was the same day I bought my special pea shooter."

"I've always wanted a pea shooter," said Hal. "I tried making one from a piece of bamboo. It wasn't much good."

Mr. Tooth nodded. "I tried that too. The peas kept getting stuck."

"That's right," said Hal. "And when I tried a thicker piece of bamboo the peas didn't go very far."

"I know what you mean, son," said the old man. "That's why I saved up and bought that special one." He shook his head and sighed. "It was a beauty. It was made out of metal and it folded down like a telescope. I could carry it in my pocket without anyone knowing."

"Wow," said Hal. "That would be great."

Mr. Tooth nodded. "It was. And the night we went to the concert I had filled my pocket with dried peas. We always had dried peas in the house. My father liked pea soup. Anyway, our seats at the concert hall were upstairs. We were seated in the front row, and even though I was quite small at the time, I could see the stage clearly through the railings. When we arrived the concert was about to begin. The orchestra was seated and waiting for the conductor to appear."

Hal waited as the old man removed his cap and rubbed his shiny bald head. Mr. Tooth nodded.

"The conductor came onto the stage and everyone clapped. I wasn't clapping. I was too busy watching a funny little man creeping along behind the conductor. When the conductor turned to bow to the audience the little man held onto his coat tails and pulled. As the conductor bent forward the little man let go of the coat. The conductor almost fell on his face. I started to giggle. My father told me to be quiet. Then he whispered to my mother that he hoped the phantom wasn't going to spoil the concert." The old man stopped and nodded slowly. "But he did."

"Why?" said Hal. "Why did this phantom do things like that?"

"Ah," said Mr. Tooth. "I forgot to tell you. Many years before, the phantom had been an oboe player in the orchestra. He was really quite good and one night he was given an important solo. Just as he was about to begin he had a fit of coughing. The second oboe player had to play the solo."

"That was rotten luck," said Hal.

"It was," agreed Mr. Tooth. "But the next time he was given a solo it happened again. You see, although he was good on the oboe he was nervous. And every time he was to perform on his own the coughing started." The old man sighed and shook his head. "So he never did play a solo and he became a very bitter old man. He saw younger members of the orchestra become soloists while he remained just another player."

"That was bad luck wasn't it," said Hal, "being nervous like that."

"It was." Mr. Tooth nodded. "But getting mad was no good. It didn't help. He just became a nasty old man. At first people had felt sorry for him. But as he became bitter, he said mean things, did mean things. And one day he was told to leave. As he left the concert hall for the last time he cursed everyone. 'I'll be back,' he shouted. 'I will be back'."

Hal waited once more as Mr. Tooth paused.

The old man stroked his moustache and then rubbed his chin. Then he continued.

"It was a year later that they learned the old man had died. When he was found he was seated at his desk. There was paper all round him, sheets and sheets of paper. On each were written only four words—I WILL BE BACK. And the very day they heard that he was gone the trouble began. At the concert that night the flute player made a mess of his solo. He said that every time he took a breath it felt as if someone was holding his nose. And he thought he heard the old man laughing. Nothing happened at the next concert or the next. Then at a concert for a visiting king, the guest soloist, a clarinet player from the king's country, kept playing wrong notes. He complained that someone held his fingers down and laughed in his ear."

Hal started to laugh. The crossing guard looked at him sternly and then smiled. He sighed. "I guess it was funny in a way. But I should tell you what happened the night I was there. The conductor recovered himself and bowed again. He turned to the orchestra and raised his hands. Just as he was about to start conducting the little old man tugged on his arm. The conductor turned angrily and as he did so the old man darted round to the other side. He pinched the conductor on his behind."

Hal started to laugh. He couldn't help it. Old Mr. Tooth was laughing too. "It was funny, but people were getting annoyed. 'What is the conductor doing?' said a woman behind me. 'Is he ill?' my mother asked." Mr. Tooth nodded. "Then I realized that no one could see the old oboe player. I had an idea. I took out my pea shooter, put a couple of peas in my mouth, and took aim. Just as the phantom was about to grab the conductor's baton I fired."

"Did you hit him?" asked Hal.

"Sure did," said Mr. Tooth. "Right on his nose."

"Wow," said Hal. "What a shot."

"Well," said the old man. "I was really aiming for his cheek. I almost missed."

"What did he do?" Hal looked up at his friend. "Did he get mad?"

"Yes he did," said Mr. Tooth. "But he waited. He didn't touch the conductor again. Instead

he crept over to the drummer. Then he looked up and pointed at me. He started to laugh." The crossing guard nodded and chuckled quietly to himself. "The next thing I knew, the orchestra was playing. But the phantom was reaching over the drummer's hand toward the cymbals. I knew I had to act. So I raised my pea shooter and fired. Just as I did so the phantom pulled back his hand. 'Ping'—the pea hit the cymbal. The conductor looked angrily over at the drummer. Then the phantom disappeared, but only for a moment. A second later I saw him standing behind the trombonist. He pointed at me again and reached out to grab the trombone. I fired again, but he was too quick. I hit the trombone player's hand and he pulled back hard making a dreadful raspberry."

Hal burst out laughing. He just couldn't help it. He could almost hear the noise.

"Hold on there," said the old man. "I haven't finished yet."

"Sorry, Mr. Tooth. But I can just see it all in my mind."

"Yes, well," the old man smiled. "The next time I saw him he was over by the bass player.

The bass player was a huge man and the phantom had climbed up on a chair behind him. He peered round the man's head and pointed at me. This time I was mad. I put five or six peas in my mouth. This time I would get him. But he was too fast. I fired— one, two, three—he was gone. But the bass player was waving his bow in the air as if he was swatting flies. He hit the tuba player, who blew an even worse raspberry than the trombone player. The phantom rushed over to the lady at the harp and I fired again. There was a terrible jangling of strings as she jumped up screaming that she'd been bitten."

Hal was now beside himself. The phantom seemed to have gained a sense of humour.

Mr. Tooth was shaking his head sadly. "The next thing I knew, my father had lifted me off my feet and was carrying me up the aisle. The hall was in an uproar. People were screaming— 'The Phantom, it's The Phantom!'."

"What happened, Mr. Tooth? Did you get into trouble?"

"Get into trouble?" The old man snorted. "I should say so. No one would believe me. And no one believed in the phantom when the story came out—not for a while at least. It was all over the front page of the newspapers. 'BOY WITH PHANTOM PEA SHOOTER PELTS PLAYERS!"

"Wow!" said Hal. "Maybe I'll be a phantom of some kind." He shook his head. "What I don't understand is, why did the pea hit him on the nose? Why didn't it go right through him?"

"Only a phantom could tell you that, son. Now off you go, here comes your dad."

CHAPTER EIGHT

The Film Director

"So, did you decide to be the phantom?" asked Mr. Tooth.

Hal shook his head. "I'm still deciding," he said.

"Well you'd best be quick, son. Two more days and it will be Hallowe'en."

"Yes, I know," said Hal. It really was beginning to feel like Hallowe'en and as he looked round he shivered. There was something ghostly in the air. The mist was thicker tonight. He couldn't see the poles of the street lights, but the yellow lights themselves looked down through the haze like giant eyes from out of space.

"Fog's thicker tonight," said the old man. He blew on his hands and rubbed them together. "Reminds me of the time the film company came to our village." He smiled. "They gave me a part."

"Did you get lots of money?" asked Hal.

Mr. Tooth shook his head. "No. In fact I was lucky to get any at all. I was only a boy at the time."

"That doesn't matter," said Hal. "Jeff, a friend of mine was in a film once, when he was six. He got more than a thousand dollars." He shook his head. "Jeff wanted to get a bike and all kinds of stuff; but his dad put all the money in the bank."

"Very sensible," said the crossing guard. "Money in the bank earns more money."

"I know," said Hal. "But even so, he could've had just one thing. All he got was new clothes, and even then he couldn't choose the special jacket he wanted."

"Special jacket." Mr. Tooth nodded. "The film director had a special jacket. In fact everything he had was special: his chair had big letters— DIRECTOR; his hat had a thick band round it with DIRECTOR on the front and back; his car had DIRECTOR painted on the doors."

"He must have been very important," said Hal.

"Hm!" snorted Mr. Tooth. "He thought he was

the most important person ever to live. Everyone ran round him as if they were scared. If he'd been a king in the old days he was the sort who would've probably had people's heads cut off, if he didn't like them. But he got it in the end."

"Got it, Mr. Tooth—what do you mean?" asked Hal.

"Well," said the old man. "He thought he was so big and clever; but the ghost of our village fooled him."

"What kind of ghost?" asked Hal.

"An ancient ghost," said Mr. Tooth. "She hadn't been seen for two or three hundred years—Lady Matilda Godyevor—she's buried in the church where I sang."

"Was she the one that rode round on a horse without clothes?" asked Hal.

Mr. Tooth chuckled. "No, son. That was Lady Winifred Godiva. Lady Matilda was Lady Winifed's cousin but she spelt her name differently."

"Why?" asked Hal.

"Why what?" said the old man.

"Why did she spell her name differently?" said Hal.

"Oh, that." Mr. Tooth smiled. "In those days people could spell things how they wanted."

"Boy, I wish we could do that," said Hal. "That would be great. But…" He paused. He wasn't sure if he should say what was on his mind.

"What is it, son?" Mr. Tooth looked down.

"Well…" Hal paused again. "It's just that this is a story about a woman ghost… and I, well… I can't be a woman ghost."

"Why not?" said Mr. Tooth. "No one would ever guess who you were. And besides, you might decide to be the film director."

"Is he a ghost then?" asked Hal.

"I wouldn't doubt it," said the crossing guard. "He died a broken man a few years later. He never completed another film after this one."

"What happened?" asked Hal.

"Listen and I'll tell you." Mr. Tooth looked up. The yellow glow from the street lights gave his face a ghostly pallor. Hal shivered. He wondered if his own face looked like that. The old man stroked his moustache. Then he began.

"As I was saying, this film director had come to the village to make a film. The film was about an ancient knight who wanted to marry Lady

Godyevor; not the naked one, the one who's buried in the church." The old man nodded and then continued. "Anyway, the story has it that this Lady came to visit Sir Thomas. It was more than just a visit really; you see, an evil knight also wanted Lady Godyevor; she was a very beautiful lady; the most beautiful in the whole place at the time."

Hal shrugged. Now he knew he couldn't be the ghost of the lady. First of all, if he told people that he was Lady Godyevor, they'd immediately think of the one on the horse. Then people would ask why he was all dressed up instead of being naked; and trying to explain about people spelling how they wanted would waste time when he was out 'trick or treating'. And anyway, the lady was beautiful.

Mr. Tooth was continuing the story. "The wicked knight was Sir Oswald Bodkin-Bodkin. He had tried to force Lady Godyevor to marry him. He'd stormed the castle where she lived and locked up her parents, Sir Horace and Lady Maud. Lady Godyevor had escaped just in time. She fled on horseback to Sir Thomas. Sir Bodkin-Bodkin was furious. He set guards on Sir

Horace and Lady Maud and all the servants at the Godyevor castle. Then he left. He knew that he couldn't fight Sir Thomas by himself, so he went to the king. He said that Sir Thomas was the one who had stormed Castle Godyevor. He asked the king to send other knights with him to rescue the lady."

"What a rotten liar," said Hal. "Did the king believe him?"

"Unfortunately he did, son." Mr. Tooth nodded. His tooth bobbed up and down on his lower lip. "Liars can often be very charming and persuasive." He breathed in deeply and pressed his lips together in a firm straight line. "He was joined by two other knights and rode with a small army to kill Sir Thomas and take Lady Godyevor.

"Sir Thomas was having dinner when they arrived. He went up on the battlements of his castle to see what could be done. He realized that the longer he waited the worse things would get. So he made a plan for a night attack. Sir Bodkin-Bodkin hadn't expected that. It was a misty night." Mr. Tooth looked around. "Something like tonight I would think." He

nodded. "So, with the mist as cover and with the suddenness of the attack, Sir Thomas took the enemy by surprise. The battle raged all night and when morning came the other knights were in full flight; except for the evil Bodkin-Bodkin."

"Was he still fighting?" asked Hal.

"Not Bodkin-Bodkin," said the old man. "That cunning, wicked knight had crept, unseen, into the castle with a small party of his most evil soldiers. He'd captured the lady and as Sir Thomas chased the last of the other knights Bodkin-Bodkin stood on the castle battlements and laughed."

"What a fink!" said Hal. "What a dirty rotten fink."

Mr. Tooth nodded. "He was rotten indeed and his evil laugh carried loud and clear through the morning air. Sir Thomas turned and realized what had happened. He was quick to act. Sir Thomas was a marksman with the long bow. He took a bow from one of his soldiers and drew an arrow. It flew, whistling through the air straight to its mark."

"Wow," said Hal. "He was good. So he hit this Sir Bodkin-Bodkin."

Mr. Tooth nodded slowly, his face grim. "That he did, son. The arrow flew straight to his chest, but…" Hal waited as the old man paused. "The arrow hit the armour of Bodkin-Bodkin. It glanced off and entered the heart of Lady Godyevor."

"Oh no!" Hal couldn't believe it.

"I'm afraid so." The old man sighed. "It was a tragedy. Sir Bodkin-Bodkin escaped even though Sir Thomas pursued him. Sir Thomas never married. He spent his life building the church where he buried Lady Godyevor—Saint Matilda's it's called."

Hal stood shaking his head. He felt really mad. The rotten knight had escaped. Then he looked up at Mr. Tooth. "That's a good story, Mr. Tooth. But I thought you said it was a ghost story."

"Well so it is, son. I had to tell you what happened so that you'd understand the rest." The old man nodded. "As I said, Sir Thomas buried Lady Godyevor and then built St. Matilda's church in her honour. When the church was finished he went there every day. He had a seat in front. Day after day he sat there until his

death. No one ever sat in that seat again—except Lady Godyevor, her ghost that is—and the film director.

"For years after the death of Sir Thomas, the ghost of Lady Godyevor was seen seated in the church. This went on until about three hundred years ago when the church was being repaired after a terrible storm. The storms in the area were famous. Every year on the anniversaries of the deaths of Lady Godyevor and Sir Thomas storms would rage—thunder, lightening, torrential rain. The storm that damaged the church was the last. The workmen found the graves of the lady and the knight shattered. They decided to bury the remains in one tomb. From then on the storms ceased and the lady was never seen again; well, not until I saw her."

Hal waited. Mr. Tooth was gazing up into the night. Hal wondered if the old man was remembering those many years ago, when he was a boy.

"It started when the director sat in Sir Thomas's seat." Mr. Tooth shook his head. "He'd been told. No one ever sat there. But he had no respect, that man. He laughed and said that he was more important than any dead

knight. 'Let the dead take care of the dead', he said. And that's what happened."

"What happened?" asked Hal.

"The Lady," said the old man. "I saw her. No one else did. The director sat in the seat, in the church with his hat on his head. Wham! She had that off. Took half his hair with it. But he still sat there. Then she put her hands over his mouth. He couldn't talk. For him that was terrible. He loved talking. But still he wouldn't move. Then she made the seat into a block of ice—and the floor all round him. He sat shivering until he was half frozen. The actors couldn't understand what was going on. But the director was determined. So she put her hands over his eyes. That did it. A film director has to see what's going on."

"So he moved," said Hal.

"Yes, he did, but not far." Mr. Tooth nodded. "He brought his own chair into the church."

"The one with DIRECTOR painted on it?" asked Hal.

"The very one," said the old man. "Placed it right next to the knight's seat."

"But why was he in the church anyway?" asked

Hal. "Why wasn't he at the castle?"

"Ah." Mr. Tooth nodded. "Firstly, the castle was in ruins; almost gone. And then he'd changed the story, as I mentioned. He called the good knight Sir Bodkin-Bodkin and had him rescue Lady Godyevor in the church, as Sir Thomas was forcing her to marry him."

"Why?" asked Hal. "That wasn't the story. Why would he do that?"

"I'll tell you in a minute," said Mr. Tooth. "As I told you, Lady Godyevor fooled him. She made the actor who was playing Sir Bodkin-Bodkin develop a twitch in one eye. Every time he smiled his eye twitched and he looked evil. And she made the actor playing Sir Thomas fall sick. He was sick for days. I had the part of his page, his servant. Anyway, one day he appeared, absolutely recovered—only it wasn't the actor—it was the ghost of the real Sir Thomas. No one else seemed to know this. I did somehow. I tried to tell the director, but he just got mad at me. He wanted to film the missing scenes and leave. He was fed up with our village." The old man smiled. "So he carried on. They finished the scenes and left the same day." The crossing guard started to laugh. "Guess what happened."

"Well," said Hal. "If they'd filmed a ghost there wouldn't be anyone on the film."

Mr. Tooth looked quite angry. "How did you know that?"

"I didn't, Mr. Tooth." Hal shrugged. "It just stands to reason. But I bet those scenes looked stupid."

The old man lost his frown. He nodded, smiling. "Can you imagine a scene with Sir Bodkin-Bodkin, his eye twitching madly, rushing down the aisle of the church and wrestling with someone who wasn't there." Mr. Tooth burst into laughter, rocking back and forth. "They came back to retake the scenes, but the actor playing Sir Thomas became sick again. Every time they went to shoot the scenes he fell sick. I knew it was because they'd changed the story, changed the names; but the director wouldn't listen."

"You said you'd tell me why he changed it," said Hal. "Why did he?"

Mr. Tooth nodded. He looked long and hard at Hal. "I think it was because his name was Bodkin-Bodkin," he said.

CHAPTER NINE
The Executioner

Hal stood at the top of the school steps. Coming out of the brightly lit hall it took a while for his eyes to adjust to the gloom. The mist was thicker than ever. He could just see Mr. Tooth standing on the sidewalk, rocking back and forth. The old man stood with his back towards Hal and from here only his head and shoulders were visible above the blanket of thick white vapour.

Hal wondered if he could cross the yard without the old man seeing him. He set off, carefully placing one foot after the other as he crept slowly towards the gate. As he came near to the fence he heard the old man singing to himself.

"With his head tucked under his arm, oh yes—with his head tucked under his arm." The crossing guard rocked back and forth on his tiny feet, rubbing his hands together briskly. The red and white 'stop' sign was leaning against the gate post.

Hal stopped in his tracks as Mr. Tooth finished his song and then approached even more carefully as the old man started to hum. He reached out slowly and lifted the 'stop' sign gently from the ground. Then he waited.

"Whooh," moaned Hal as the old man stopped humming. "Whooh."

The crossing guard stood still as a statue. Then slowly he turned.

Hal poked the 'stop' sign out from behind the gate post and waved it around. "Whooh. Whooh," he chanted.

Mr. Tooth started to chuckle. "You young devil," he said. "Almost scared the daylights out of me."

Hal came out from behind the post, grinning. "Did it really scare you, Mr. Tooth?"

"Sure did, son." The old man nodded. "For a second or two. Then I realized that you'd be out at any moment." He smiled. "So, what's the decision? You don't want to be the hairy hands. I've got a feeling that you don't want to be a lady ghost; so the Lady in Black and Lady Godyevor are out. You can't be the bear. What does that leave us?"

"There's the Phantom of the Orchestra, the Film Director and the Bell Ringer," said Hal.

"Right," said Mr. Tooth. "I'd forgotten the Bell Ringer."

"Well, I can't be the Bell Ringer," replied Hal. "He hasn't got a head."

"That doesn't matter," said the crossing guard. "You can cut a cardboard box to fit over your head and just over your shoulders. Punch a couple of eye-holes in the front to see out of."

"Hey, that would be good," said Hal. "But what about the long black cloak and the hood?"

"Does your father have a raincoat, an old overcoat?

Hal nodded. "He has a dark blue raincoat. It's far too big for me though."

Mr. Tooth smiled. "It sounds perfect. With the box over your head it would probably just reach to the ground."

Hal nodded excitedly. "And I could carry the old brass bell Dad has in his study and…" He paused.

"What's the matter?" asked the old man.

"Where do I put my hands?" said Hal. "I have to be able to hold my bag and take the candies."

"Right." Mr. Tooth stroked his moustache. "I've got it. Most of those raincoats have double pockets. You can reach through a slit to the inside. If you can reach inside you can reach outside. And you can stuff the arms of the raincoat and fold them over the middle. With a pair of gloves it will look like a monk praying as he walks."

"Wow!" Hal was getting really excited. Then he thought about the bell.

It was if Mr. Tooth had read his thoughts. "But you won't be able to carry the bell—too awkward." He rocked back and forth. "Hm. Headless ghost. That would be good. It reminds me of the executioner."

"Is this another story, Mr. Tooth?" asked Hal.

"It is, son." The crossing guard peered into the mist. "I don't know if I've time to tell you though. Your father should be here soon."

Hal looked down the road. He couldn't see a thing. There was the faint noise of an engine. As it grew louder a pair of headlights loomed up and as quickly were gone as a small truck sped past.

"Going much too fast," said Mr. Tooth. "Some people shouldn't be allowed on the road." He sighed and looked down at Hal. "You just be careful tomorrow night."

"Don't you worry, Mr. Tooth. I will," said Hal. "If you're quick, maybe you could tell me the story."

"Ha! Like my stories do you. Okay," said the old man, "the executioner it is." He took a deep breath. "It was the last time I was back in England. I was on holiday, by myself, with all the time in the world. I'd hired a car and just drove from place to place without any real plan. It was springtime and on this particular day I was driving along a twisting country road. I had no idea where I was." The old man paused. "I was hungry and as I rounded a bend I came upon an old pub. It was called 'The Executioner'. A sign hung from a pole stretching out above the entrance. On it was painted a man dressed in black, a mask over his eyes, an axe grasped in his hands." Mr. Tooth nodded slowly. "The eyes of the executioner seemed to look straight at me as I got out of the car. I was in two minds about staying."

"Why did you?" asked Hal.

"I told you, son. I was hungry." Mr. Tooth breathed in heavily. "In fact, I couldn't remember ever being as hungry as I was then. So I went into the inn. It was a lovely old place: dark wood beams, copper and brass fittings, highly polished, and a welcome fire in the hearth. And behind the bar was a jovial looking man wearing a blue and white striped apron. He was the owner and a fine host. In next to no time I had beef sandwiches, cheese, and various pickles to choose from and soon I was feeling sleepy. The innkeeper woke me from a doze. 'Too fine a day to sleep, sir.' I agreed with him. But I didn't think it would be good to drive straight away. A walk would wake me up. When the innkeeper suggested I visit the castle nearby I set off, following his directions.

"It was a lovely day. The road to the castle wound through a wooded area. There were bluebells everywhere and all was still, silent." Mr. Tooth nodded. "I became aware of the silence, slowly at first and then almost as if the silence were in fact a noise. There were no sounds of birds, no scurrying of woodland creatures, nothing to break the still quiet except my own footsteps. There was an eerie feeling in the air. I was about to turn back, but rounding a bend the splendour of the castle was spread before me. Here all was quiet too. Not a ripple disturbed the surface of the moat between the patches of water lilies. Again I had second thoughts, but I was there. So I crossed the drawbridge.

"The castle was not built of stone like those of the Romans and Normans. It was built of deep red bricks. So I knew that it must have been built at the time of Henry the Eighth."

"I've heard of him," said Hal. "He's the one that had eight wives and had their heads cut off."

"Actually he had six wives," said the old man. "And he didn't have them all beheaded, only two."

"What did he do with the others?" asked Hal.

"He divorced two," said the Mr. Tooth. "One died and the last one outlived him. A lot of people think he had them all beheaded. Anyway, if you keep asking questions I'll never finish this story." The crossing guard continued.

"I was standing in the courtyard. I looked round for a guide, but the place seemed to be deserted. I called out several times and was about to leave when I heard slow, heavy footsteps. There was a door to my right and as I turned a costumed figure came striding out. He was dressed from head to foot in black. He had only one eye which stared unwinking from a single hole in his mask."

"Boy, I bet that was scary," said Hal. "Was he carrying an axe?"

"He was," said Mr. Tooth. "And I must admit, I was scared at first. But, then he asked if I was there to tour the castle. I told him I was and he led the way into the entrance hall. It was lined with oak panels. There were antique weapons: swords, pikes, double-headed axes. I shivered. It was cool in the hall, but seeing the weapons made me think of all the people that had died in bloody battles hundreds of years before. The guide was staring at me. His pale blue eye gleamed through the single slit in his mask. I felt strangely uncomfortable. I thought a joke might help and asked if there were any ghosts in the castle."

Mr. Tooth paused and shook his head. "The eye behind the mask seemed to turn paler, glinted, icy. And the executioner's fingers tightened round the handle of the axe. 'You don't believe in ghosts do you sir?' he said. Well, as you know, I do believe in ghosts. But before I could reply he continued. 'All you tourists are the same. Have to ask about ghosts.' I tried to explain but I found that I couldn't speak. The eye became paler still and I felt very cold. 'You've offended me, sir.' His voice was almost a whisper. 'Now if you will excuse me, I will ask my wife to take you on the tour.' He turned. 'She will be with you in a minute.' Then he strode off down the hall and placed his head in the crook of his right arm."

"Wow!" exclaimed Hal. "You mean he took his head off while you watched?

He sure did," said Mr. Tooth. Lifted it right off and tucked it under his arm."

"Boy, I think I might try that with that old vampire mask I've got." Hal could imagine calling at a house and pretending to lift his head off. "What was his wife like?" he asked.

"I don't know." Mr. Tooth shook his head.

"The next thing I remember was waking up on the grass beyond the castle moat. I was cold, chilled to the bone. It was dusk. Through the mist the moon rose pale above the castle, like the eye of the executioner."

Despite himself, Hal shivered. The gleaming eye of the ghost bothered him. "What did you do?" he whispered.

"Ran," said the old man. "I ran as fast as my legs would carry me, through the woods and back to the inn. When at last I staggered to my car I felt better. But then I heard those heavy footsteps again. I looked round and my eyes were drawn to the inn sign. It swung slowly above me and the executioner stared down. I knew there had been two eyes before, but now he only had one, a single eye staring down at me."

"Wow. Did you drive off Mr. Tooth? I would've."

"No son, I couldn't." The old man paused. "Before I could move a huge hand descended on my shoulder. I turned. There behind me was a man dressed in black."

Hal held his breath. Mr. Tooth nodded and then continued. "It was a policeman. I tell you, I nearly fainted. 'Can I help you, sir?' asked the policeman. I shook my head and told him that I would be fine. I couldn't think how I, a ghost hunter, could ever have been so scared. I decided to get a drink and maybe stay at the inn. I wanted to lay this ghost to bed. 'Where are you going, sir?' the policeman asked. I told him. 'Ho, ho, ho.' The policeman laughed and shook his head. 'The inn's been closed for years sir, ever since old Jack drowned in the castle moat. They reckon he saw the executioner."

Hal stared at the crossing guard. "You mean, the innkeeper was a ghost too?"

Mr. Tooth nodded. He chuckled and his tooth bobbed up and down. "Even though I'd seen many a ghost, that day really got to me. I was away from there as fast as I could. I tried to find the place again the next day, just to get it out of my mind. I never could find it." He shook his head.

Hal stared up at the old man. Mr. Tooth suddenly looked tired and old. He didn't look as if he had much to eat either. Hal decided to bring some of his candy to share with the crossing guard after Hallowe'en. He was about to ask Mr.

Tooth if he could eat candy, with his tooth bobbing up and down, when he heard a car horn. A moment later his father drove up.

CHAPTER TEN
All Hallows Eve

"See you tonight, son."

Hal climbed out of the car. "Can you come earlier tonight, Dad?"

"I'll try, Hal. Maybe I can make a call across town. Now, off you go. Have a good day."

Hal shut the car door and slung his bag over his shoulder. He was excited. His father's raincoat was perfect and his mother had helped make a hood from some old black cloth in the rag basket. The hood was mounted on top of the cardboard box with wire from a clothes hanger. Mike had helped with that; and the box was covered with one of Mike's old blue tee shirts. The effect was eerie. When Hal stood in the dark and Dad switched on his flashlight, Hal looked just like an ancient monk gliding along without his head. And the old mask, tied onto a

98

stuffed plastic bag and tucked under the arm of the raincoat, looked gruesome.

Hal smiled contentedly. This was going to be a great Hallowe'en. A real ghost would be walking the streets tonight. He wished he could go out by himself, but his father insisted that he go with Mike. His brother was going as a rock singer. He had reflector tape all over his shirt. He'd covered his shoes with it too, and tied strips of tape to his guitar. Mike would carry the flashlight. Hal ran up the steps and entered the school.

At four o'clock Hal stood on the steps once more. The other children had gone and he waited impatiently for his father. There was no sign of Mr. Tooth either.

Gradually it became dark and as it had over the past two weeks, the mist began to form, at first in thin wisps, then in thick gray-white clouds rolling across the yard. Hal shivered and zipped up his coat. Then he heard the singing.

"With his head tucked under his arm, oh yes... With his head tucked under his arm." It was Mr. Tooth.

Hal peered through the mist. He couldn't see

the old man. He ran down the steps two at a time and ran to the school gate. There was Mr. Tooth leaning against the post. "Well, hi there," he said. "I wondered where you'd got to."

"I couldn't see you," said Hal. He put his bag on the ground.

"Couldn't see me?" The crossing guard laughed. "I've been here all the time. It's my job. And a very important one on Hallowe'en night too. Many a dreadful accident has happened on Hallowe'en night. I hope you'll be careful."

"I will, Mr. Tooth," said Hal. "My brother Mike's coming with me." Hal explained how Mike would be dressed. "And your idea about the box on my head is brilliant. Thanks, Mr. Tooth."

The crossing guard chuckled. "Glad to be of help, son." He laughed again. "You'll be the best one out there tonight—if you don't run into a real ghost of course."

Hal looked at the old man. He shook his head. "You had me going with some of your stories, Mr. Tooth. But Mike says there aren't any ghosts, they're just in a person's imagination."

"Maybe in some people's, son." The crossing guard rocked back and forth on his tiny feet. "But remember what I told you. Some people hear them; some people feel them; but other people really do see ghosts." He paused, his mouth open, the false tooth resting on his lip. "Is that your dad's car I hear?"

Hal listened. In the distance he could hear an engine. It did sound like Dad's car. But the mist was so thick that he couldn't see the headlights yet.

"Why is he coming from the other direction?" asked the old man. "He's earlier than usual, isn't he?"

"He said he might make a call across town," said Hal. "That way he could be earlier. I asked him."

"The crossing guard nodded. "Good dad you've got there." He turned and picked up his 'stop' sign from where it rested against the gate post. "Come on, I'll see you across the road."

Hal picked up his bag and walked beside the old man. They were half way across the road when there was a screech of tires and the roar of an engine. Hal stood as if frozen to the spot. Mr.

Tooth turned, grabbed Hal by the shoulders, and thrust him in front of him. "Run, Hal," he shouted. "Run!"

Hal felt himself propelled forward and tripped over the curb at the side of the road. The truck was right there behind him, lights blazing. Then he heard the screech of tires once more, as the driver applied the brakes. There was a dull thump, a piercing cry of agony. The crossing guard's sign skidded across the sidewalk as the truck roared into life and sped off.

Hal realized that car headlights now lighted the area where he lay. A door opened. Running feet approached. "Hal! Hal! Are you alright?" His father bent over him. "That driver should be taken off the road, overtaking on a night like this."

Hal started to sob. "He hit Mr. Tooth, Dad. Mr. Tooth saved me and he killed him."

Hal's father groaned. "Oh no." He turned. "Maybe he's not dead. Maybe he's only hurt."

Hal shook his head. "He's dead, Dad. I know he is." He got up and stood looking into the road. The headlights from the car showed nothing. The engine purred gently. There was no other sound. Hal's father searched the area quickly. "We'd better phone the police. Is there anyone still in the school?"

Hal looked across the road. A light glowed in the principal's office. "I think Mrs. Smith may still be there, Dad." He sniffed and wiped his eyes.

"Come on then." His father took his hand. As he did so, Hal bent down and picked up the 'stop' sign. They crossed the road and raced across the yard. His father let go Hal's hand and dashed up the steps two at time. Hal followed and ran down the hallway.

His father was talking to the principal as Hal rushed into the office.

"Did you say a truck hit the school crossing guard?" asked the principal.

"That's right," said Hal's father. "He was showing my son across the road. I must use the phone and call the police."

"We..." the principal paused. "We don't have a crossing guard any more," she said slowly. "Not since they put in the traffic lights a year ago."

Hal looked at the teacher. He couldn't believe what he was hearing. "But..." he shook his head. He could hear Mr. Tooth's voice. 'Run, Hal.

Run!' How had Mr. Tooth known his name? He'd never told him.

The teacher was smiling at him, waiting. His father was looking confused. Hal continued. "I've talked with him, every night for the last two weeks. He said I could call him Mr. Tooth—everyone does." He stared at the principal. Her mouth had dropped open and her face was white.

"Did you say 'Mr. Tooth'?" she whispered.

Hal nodded. "He helped me decide what to wear for Hallowe'en."

The teacher shook her head slowly. When she spoke her voice trembled. "There was a crossing guard that we called Mr. Tooth. It was years ago. He was killed on Hallowe'en night saving a student from this school." She sighed. "Dear old Mr. Tooth. He loved children."

Hal looked down at the sign in his hand. He'd almost expected it to have disappeared. He gripped it tightly. Some people hear ghosts and some feel them: he'd seen a ghost and heard one too. He'd never forget the tales of Mr. Tooth.